For my parents – WDT

First published in 2015 by Fat Fox Books Ltd.

Fox's Den, Wickets, Frittenden Road, Staplehurst, Kent TN12 0DH.
www.fatfoxbooks.com

ISBN: 978-0992872847

Fat Fox and associated logos are trademarks and/or registered
trademarks of Fat Fox Books Ltd.

Text and illustrations copyright © Wen Dee Tan 2015.

The right of Wen Dee Tan to be identified as the author and as the
illustrator of this work has been asserted.

A CIP catalogue record for this book is available from the British Library.

Printed and bound in China.

Wen Dee Tan

Winner of Macmillan Prize 2013, third place

fatfoxbooks.com

Once upon a time in a village
there lived an ordinary girl named Lili.

Well, ordinary except for one thing...

Lili had RED-HOT hair.

So hot that it burned
everything it touched.

Sometimes it's small.

Sometimes it's BIG.

Lili was helpful to
her family

throughout the seasons
(especially winter).

But not all her neighbours
thought so.

Lili found it hard to make friends.

Eventually, the village children
didn't want to play
with her anymore.

So, Lili found other ways of amusing herself that didn't need other people,

like drawing

and fruit picking
in the woods.

Until one day, she stumbled
upon some village children
lost in the woods.

Brave Lili ran to help.

It was getting dark,
but Lili lit up the way...

and led them safely home.

And Lili finally made
some real friends.